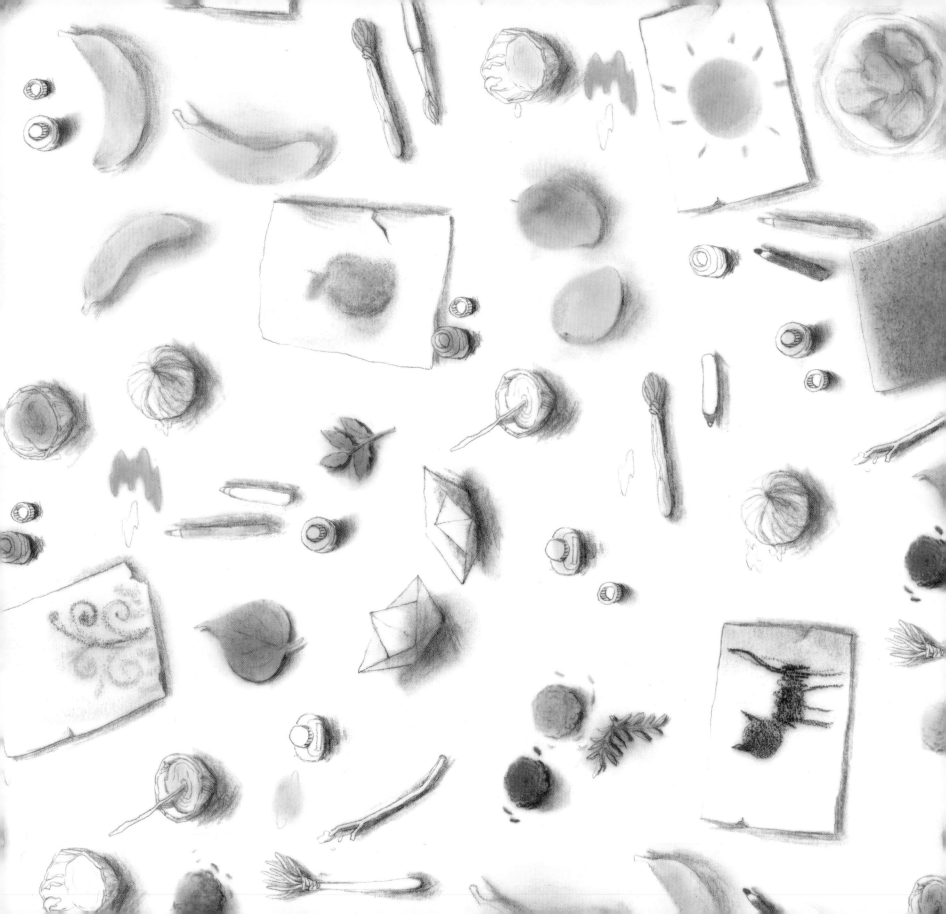

# DADAJI'S Paintbrush

This is an Arthur A. Levine book
Published by Levine Querido

## LQ

LEVINE QUERIDO

www.levinequerido.com · info@levinequerido.com

Levine Querido is distributed by Chronicle Books, LLC

Text and illustrations copyright © 2022 by Rashmi Sirdeshpande
Illustrations copyright © 2022 by Ruchi Mhasane

Originally published in the U.K. by Andersen Press

Library of Congress Control Number: 2022931611

ISBN 978-1-64614-172-2

Printed and bound in China

MIX
Paper from
responsible sources
FSC
www.fsc.org
FSC™ C104723

Published in August 2022
First Printing

The text type was set in ITC Clearface.

Ruchi Mhasane created her illustrations using colour pencils and pastels
on paper, a digital lightbox, and the inspiration of the western
Konkan coast of India where Rashmi's family is from.

# DADAJI's Paintbrush

RASHMI SIRDESHPANDE

RUCHI MHASANE

WITHDRAWN

LQ
LEVINE QUERIDO

MONTCLAIR • AMSTERDAM • HOBOKEN

Once, in a tiny village in India, there was a boy who loved to paint. He lived with his grandfather in an old house full of paintings.

First, the boy painted with his fingers. He printed with marigolds, betel leaves, and coconut shells.

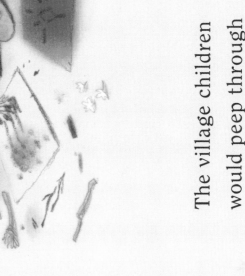

As he got bigger, he painted with brushes made of sticks. They had strips of cloth, reeds, or jasmine flowers wrapped around the ends.

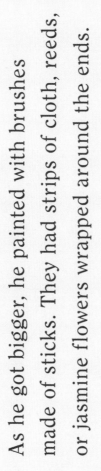

The village children would peep through the windows to watch them paint.

Sometimes, the boy's grandfather would invite them to join in.

The boy and his grandfather did everything together.
They grew bananas, pineapples, and jackfruit, and
sold them in the local market....

shared sticky, juicy mangoes with
the village children…

and made paper boats for them to float down the street in the
monsoon rain. They read books and picked out what they'd
paint the next day.

When the rains had gone, every night, they would be on their rooftop beds and watch the stars until they fell asleep.

They didn't have much, but they had each other.

"Don't ever leave me," the boy would say.

"I won't," his grandfather would reply, holding the boy so tight that his bones would hurt…

...but one day, he did.

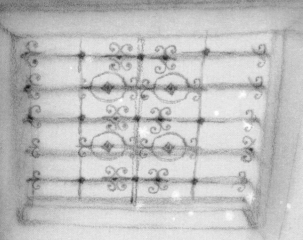

All that was left of his grandfather was
the old house full of paintings. Soon
after, the boy stood at his desk.
He noticed a little box wrapped in string, with
a note that read: "From Dadaji, with love."
Inside was his grandfather's best paintbrush.

At first, the boy didn't touch it. He couldn't. He wouldn't. When he tried to look at it, his chest ached.

So, one day, he put it up on a shelf so high he had to get up on his toes to reach it.

Days and months passed by.
Seasons changed.
The boy forgot all about the box.
Or at least, he tried to.

But mangoes didn't taste the
same anymore.
At night, the stars didn't
sparkle the way they used to.
When the rains arrived
again, there was no one
to make paper boats with.

The village children didn't visit anymore either. The house felt empty. Like the hole in the boy's heart where his grandfather used to be.

Where all the colours used to be.

Finally, the boy took all the paintings and locked them away. In time, the paints dried up and the box and the paintings gathered dust.

But then, one day,
a small girl turned
up at the boy's
door. She held a
stick with reeds
wrapped around
the end.

"Please teach me how to paint," she said. "Like your dadaji taught my mummy."

The boy shook his head, but the girl wouldn't leave. "Oh please," she said.

So, he mixed up some paints and found her a fresh sheet of paper.

The girl plunged her brush into the paints and dotted the page with bright blue and green splodges. Then, she stopped and frowned. "It's no good," she said. "This was a bad idea. I can't do it..."

She was about to give up when the boy said, "Wait…"
There was always a way.

He looked closely at the page. Then he remembered.
Then he smiled.

The boy unlocked
the door at the back
of the house and
showed the girl
his grandfather's
paintings.

If they looked closely, in the background of every painting, they could see little splodges of paint. Sometimes made with fingers, sometimes with brushes made of sticks, reeds, and flowers.

Together, the boy and his grandfather had turned every one of them into something wonderful.

All it took was time and attention.

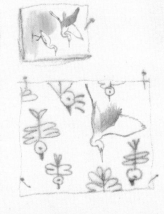

And so the boy reached for the box, took out his grandfather's paintbrush, and started to paint.

The girl watched and copied. They painted together every day, and, as time passed by, the house was filled with colour again.

The boy has been painting ever since.

Sometimes, the village children peep through the window to watch. Sometimes they paint, they laugh, and the boy makes paper boats for them to float away down the street in the monsoon rain.

He knows in his heart that his grandfather will always be with him.

## AUTHOR'S NOTE

This story is a blend of so many different things, but at its heart, it's inspired by my love for my grandfather and his love for me. He didn't talk about it. He didn't have to. Whenever it was time for me to go back to England after visiting him in Goa, India, he would hold me so tight that my bones hurt. You might remember that line in the book. That's him. He isn't around anymore, but that feeling that the people you love will always, always be with you? That's just how I feel.

The rest of the story is based on my father. He's not a painter, but he loves the arts, and he's a kind, generous soul who gives so much to the community. The book is based on his childhood in Goa (and to some extent mine too!)— not the painting but the paper boats, the fruits, the market, and the monsoon rain. It just so happened that Ruchi is from a similar part of India. And so the stunning setting in her artwork is *just* like our home in Goa—right down to the veranda, the rooftops, and all that beautiful greenery! Can you imagine how amazing it was to first see those pictures and realize that although we never once discussed it, Ruchi had painted everything that was inside my heart? How does that even happen?

There's so much in this book that I believe in. I believe that there are no mistakes in art and that every single one of us should just feel free to play and create. I believe little things bring so much happiness—like sharing juicy mangoes, or a story, or watching the stars. And I believe love is something that lives on forever and ever. I've put all of these things inside this little story and Ruchi has brought it to life in a way I could never have imagined. I love what we have created and I hope you will too.

*In loving memory of my grandfather,*
*Shri Laxmikant Desai*

*—RS*

*To Aaji-Abba and Aaji-Anna,*
*with whom I wish I had more time*

*—RM*

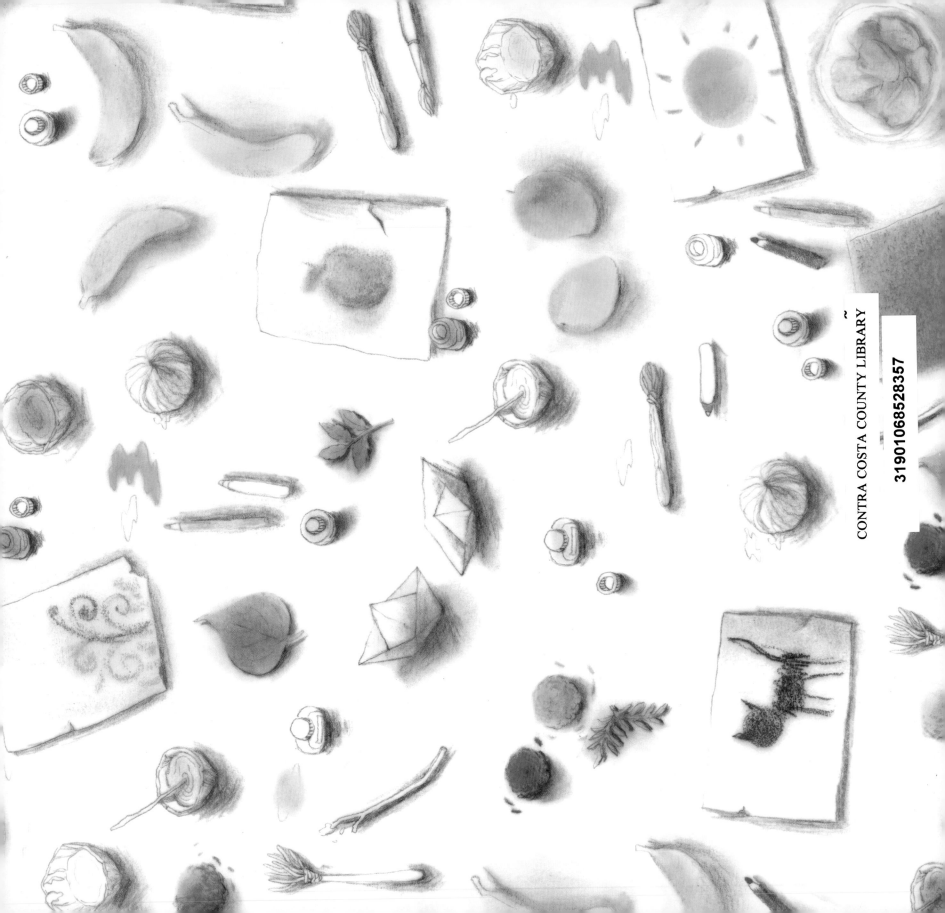